Artwork by Julie Paschkis

Calvin Coconut
KUNG FOOEY

Other Books About
Calvin Coconut

TROUBLE MAGNET

THE ZIPPY FIX

DOG HEAVEN

ZOO BREATH

HERO OF HAWAII

Calvin Coconut

KUNG FOOEY

Graham Salisbury

illustrated by

Jacqueline Rogers

WENDY
LAMB
BOOKS

Text copyright © 2011 by Graham Salisbury
Cover art and interior illustrations copyright © 2011 by Jacqueline Rogers

All rights reserved. Published in the United States by Wendy Lamb Books, an imprint of Random House Children's Books, a division of Random House, Inc., New York.

Wendy Lamb Books and the colophon are trademarks of Random House, Inc.

Visit us on the Web! www.randomhouse.com/kids

Educators and librarians, for a variety of teaching tools, visit us at www.randomhouse.com/teachers

Library of Congress Cataloging-in-Publication Data
Salisbury, Graham.
Calvin Coconut : kung fooey / Graham Salisbury ; [illustrations by Jacqueline Rogers]. – 1st ed.
p. cm.
ISBN 978-0-385-73963-4 (trade) – ISBN 978-0-385-90797-2 (lib. bdg.) –
ISBN 978-0-375-89796-2 (ebook) – ISBN 978-0-375-86506-0 (pbk.) [1. Interpersonal relations–Fiction. 2. Automobile driving–Fiction. 3. Schools–Fiction. 4. Family life–Hawaii–Fiction. 5. Hawaii–Fiction.] I. Rogers, Jacqueline, ill. II. Title.
III. Title: Kung fooey.
PZ7.S15225Cadk 2011
[Fic]–dc22
2010029415

Printed in the United States of America

10 9 8 7 6 5 4 3 2 1

First Edition

For Keenan
Honor your life
Be the best you can be
—G.S.

For Wendy
—J.R.

1

KUNG FU

One morning I slid off my top bunk and staggered over to the wall to measure myself. Maybe I'd grown overnight.

I grabbed a book and pencil, and made a mark.

"Aaack!"

My sleepy dog, Streak, leaped off the

bottom bunk and ran around the room barking. What's up? What's up? What's up?

"Aaaaaaaack!" I screamed again.

I burst out of my room.

"Mom! Mom!" I shouted, stumbling into the kitchen from my bedroom in the garage. "Something's wrong!"

Mom grabbed my shoulders. "Settle down, Calvin, settle down." Her face was a frown of concern. "Now . . . what's wrong?"

"I'm shrinking, Mom! For real! I measured myself and–"

"Shrinking." It wasn't a question. She raised an eyebrow.

"Yeah, Mom, I'm getting *smaller,* not bigger."

My six-year-old sister, Darci, sat frozen at the breakfast counter gaping at me, her spoon dripping milk into her cereal bowl. Stella, the tenth-grader who had come to live with us to help Mom, stood at the kitchen sink with her back to us. She didn't care that I was shrinking to death. She didn't even turn around.

Mom let go and brushed dog hair off my T-shirt. "What makes you think you're shrinking, Calvin?"

"Well . . . I . . . I, uh . . ."

Calm down. Breathe.

I gulped. "I just measured myself on the wall in my room and I'm . . . I'm an inch shorter than I was last week. I'm not kidding, Mom, there's something wrong with me . . . and . . . and . . ."

Maybe I was dying. Maybe my time was up.

I took a deep breath.

Mom tried really hard not to smile. "There must be some mistake, Cal. People don't just go around getting smaller."

Stella spurted out a laugh and staggered away from the sink.

Mom turned to look at her. "Stella," she said, and left the word hanging—which was Mom's way of hinting that laughing at a shrinking person wasn't very nice.

Stella bent over, holding her stomach, laughing and laughing.

"Stop!" I said. "I'm . . . disappearing, and that's not funny!"

Stella's eyes were wet with tears. She pointed at me, trying to speak, but couldn't. My shrinking problem was the funniest thing she'd ever heard in her entire life.

"Well, I am!" I said to her. "You'd be worried, too, if you were getting smaller!"

Mom studied Stella. "Stella, did you . . . ?"

Stella tried to stop laughing but burst out again, even louder than before.

Mom cupped the side of my face with her hand. "I think Stella just got you, sweetie."

"Huh?"

Stella ripped off a paper towel and dabbed at her eyes. Her shoulders bounced as she laughed. "Oh, oh, oh! This is just too *good*."

Mom bent close and whispered, "Stella played a trick. I think she added a line to your measuring chart. You're not shrinking."

"A . . . what?"

"An extra line. Above the *real* mark. So it looks like you shrunk."

Heat flushed over my face. I squinted at Stella. "I'll get you. I'm not kidding. You better watch out."

Stella laughed until she choked on her own spit. "Anyone could fool you, Stump. Anyone!"

"Yeah, well, you drive like an idiot and everyone laughs at you!"

That wasn't a very good comeback, but it was all I could think of. Stella was trying to get her driver's license. She already had her permit. Mom and Stella's boyfriend, Clarence, were teaching her how to drive.

"Lame," she said. "Really, really lame."

That was just the beginning of a truly strange day.

Before lunch at school that day, right in the middle of our silent reading time in Mr. Purdy's class, this new kid walked in with Mrs. Leonard, the principal.

I looked up.

Whoa!

I stopped breathing.

The whole class did.

The new kid looked us over, his eyes scrunched.

His black hair was long on top and shaved on the sides. He wore baggy black pants bunched at the top of shiny black army boots. An untucked, unbuttoned long-sleeved shirt hung over an army-colored T-shirt, and hanging over the T-shirt was a chain with a red-eyed black skull.

You could hear ants scratching out their homework over by the lunch boxes. You could hear our pet centipede Manly Stanley's hundred legs sliding to a halt in his sandy resort. You could hear the classroom clock ticking.

Mrs. Leonard waved to Mr. Purdy.

Mr. Purdy closed the book he was reading over his finger and stood. "Good morning, Mrs. Leonard. Who do we have here?"

Mrs. Leonard smiled. "This

is Benny Obi, Mr. Purdy, a new student who will be in your class."

Mrs. Leonard nudged the kid toward the front of the room.

The new kid took one step and stopped.

Mrs. Leonard put a hand on his shoulder. "Benny's family just moved to Kailua from Hilo. Hilo is on the Big Island, children. I'm sure you will all welcome Benny and show him around our school. Am I right?"

"Yes, Mrs. Leonard," everyone said.

Everyone but me.

I was still trying to figure out what I was looking at.

Mr. Purdy tucked his book under his arm and walked over to Mrs. Leonard and the new kid. "Welcome to fourth-grade boot camp, Benny."

The kid looked up at Mr. Purdy.

Mr. Purdy grinned, as if he was waiting for the kid to say something like, Boot camp? Cool. I like it.

But he didn't.

Mrs. Leonard nudged him toward our gaping faces. "Tell the class something about yourself, Benny."

The new kid's squinty eyes dared anyone to make even a peep.

"I know kung fu," he said.

Yow.

2

Benny Obi

Mr. Purdy pointed to the one vacant desk in our classroom. It was in the back row, right next to my friend Julio Reyes, who lived on the same street as me.

"Sit there, Benny. If you have any questions just ask Julio."

Benny gave Julio a sideways glance.

Julio stared at his desk.

Benny slid into his seat and sat stone still. A lizard on the wall.

Mrs. Leonard sighed and left.

Julio didn't say a word. Just sat looking like he'd accidentally swallowed a fly that had flown into his mouth.

The rest of the morning was eerily quiet. Benny Obi was like a firecracker with a fuse that had burned down to the powder but hadn't gone off . . . and no one wanted to check it because it might explode in your face.

After lunch, I was lounging on the grass near our classroom with my friends Julio, Willy Wolf, Rubin Tomioka, and Maya Medeiros. The sun was breathing its hot breath down our necks, but who cared? We had bigger stuff to deal with. The new kid was giving us the creeps.

And Julio had to sit next to him.

Which put him in a bad mood.

"How come Mr. Purdy put that new kid next to me? What did I do?"

Willy shook his head. "He sure is strange."

"Like from another planet," Rubin added.

"Look," Maya said, pointing with her chin toward the cafeteria.

We all turned. Benny Obi was leaning against the wall in the shade. Alone. Wearing dark glasses with mirror lenses.

"Looks like a cop," Rubin said.

Maya squinted in the sun. "Stands out, doesn't he?"

Julio humphed. "He *wants* to stand out. He's in love with himself."

I spurted out a laugh. "In love with himself?"

"Look at him," Julio spat. "Thinks he's a movie star. Who wears dark glasses at school?"

"Tito."

Julio snorted. "Two of a kind."

Tito Andrade was a sixth grader, a bully who gave us a hard time and stole stuff from us. He also thought every girl on the planet was in love with him.

I picked up a pebble and tossed it. "Maybe the new kid's nice, Julio. Who knows? He just got here. Give him a chance."

Julio glared at me. "You better watch your mouth."

"What? Why?"

"Because I know kung fu."

We all cracked up. What a line: I know kung fu.

I shook my head. Kung fu is a serious

martial art, not something you go around bragging about.

Maya slapped my arm.

"Shhh! He's coming."

We went silent as Benny Obi strolled over to us.

He stood with his hands in the pockets of his baggy black pants. "This where you folks hang out?"

For a few seconds, no one spoke.

"Well, is it?"

"Uh . . . not really," I finally said. "We, uh, we sit all over the place."

Benny Obi nodded.

"Who's the kid got Coconut for a last name? I heard he was in our class and he's related to Little Johnny Coconut, the singer in Las Vegas."

Everyone turned to me.

"That's . . . my dad," I said.

In Benny's glasses I could see the mirror image of us sitting around looking back at him.

Benny thought for a mo-
ment. "How come he's
there and you're here?"

Mind your own busi-
ness, I wanted to say.
"He and my mom got di-
vorced."

Benny bit his lower lip
and looked down. "Mines,
too."

He squatted and sat on
his heels with his arms over his
knees. "You guys ever seen a human skull?"

Wow. What kind of a question was *that*?

Everyone shook their head.

"Well, I have," Benny said. "I found it in a
lava tube. Up by the volcano. Secret place I
discovered. You ever been in a lava tube? You
can't go in unless you have a ball of string. If
you don't have string to lead you back out,
you could get lost and never come out and you
could die of starvation. You know how long it

takes for your body to rot? You ever thought of how it might feel to have rats and mongooses eat you alive?"

What?

No one answered.

Benny grinned. "I figure that's what happened to whoever's skull that was. Could have been from new times or from old times, somebody lost, trying to find their way out. Or maybe it was a human sacrifice from the olden days. You can't tell without testing it. They can do that, you know . . . tell how old bones are. But that was the weird thing. When I found the skull there *were* no bones. Just the head. Maybe it was *obakes*."

"Ghosts," Rubin whispered, his eyes wide.

We looked at each other. We all knew the Japanese word for *ghosts*. "*Bad* ghosts," Benny Obi whispered.

Then he turned toward the rest of us. I could see my reflection gaping back at me from his glasses.

I closed my mouth.

Benny wasn't done.

"I know a kid with one and a half legs. Got attacked by a shark. A fisherman caught that shark by accident a couple days later, and when they cut the shark open they found the kid's leg in the stomach. It was still in pretty good shape, so they found the kid and gave him his leg back. The doctors sewed it on again, but it didn't work, so they took it off. Now the kid got a fake leg. You ever seen a fake leg? Steel thing with a shoe on the end? If you have long pants on you can't tell it's fake. But you can if you got shorts. I guess if you only got half a leg you don't care, ah? At least you can walk."

Benny Obi stopped talking and nodded. Then he went on. "Was me, I wouldn't care. How's about you? You ever seen a fake leg?"

He looked at us, waiting.

Uh . . .

"Well," I said. "If . . . if . . ."

I had no idea what to say.

Benny Obi stood and looked down at us.

"You guys collect stuff? I collect everything. You name it, I got it. Old books, stamps, coins, rocks, insects, Star Wars figures, Micro Machines, manga—"

"Manga?" Rubin said. "I got sixty-eight books."

"Yeah? I got like two, three hundred, maybe a thousand. I don't know, I haven't counted them up."

He looked over his shoulder at the playground. "Hey, been nice. Gotta go. See you in class. What's with the teacher, anyway? He some kind of army guy, or what? What's with the boot camp? Ain't that kind of weird?"

When nobody said anything, Benny Obi shrugged and walked away.

"Holy bazooks," I whispered.

Julio spat. "Would you want to sit next to *that*?"

3

Smoke and Squeal

After school I grabbed Darci from her first-grade room, then met up with Julio, Rubin, Willy, and Maya, who were waiting for us under a monkeypod tree. Most days we walked home together. We lived in the same neighborhood, except for Rubin, who lived halfway between us and the school.

As we headed down the quiet street, Darci tugged on my shirt. "Who's the boy in the dark glasses? Is he new? I saw you talking to him."

Julio snorted. "That's Captain Strange."

"His name is Benny, Darce. He's—"

Eeeeooooop!

All of us leaped and crashed into each other, trying to get out of the way of the horn-blast of a truck bearing down behind us. I ended up in somebody's hibiscus hedge with Julio and Darci.

We looked back out.

It wasn't a truck.

Benny Obi lifted his dark glasses as he cruised past us on his silver-and-red bike. A giant air horn was bolted to its handlebar. Benny flicked his eyebrows, dropped his glasses back onto his nose, and gave the horn another blast.

Eeeeooooop!

"Got it off my uncle," he called. "Traded him a machete for it."

He sailed on by without looking back.

Me, Julio, and Darci untangled ourselves from the hedge.

"I'm going to give that guy a wedgie," Julio said.

I laughed. "Yeah? How?"

Julio scowled. "Hire Tito."

"That would do it."

Rubin peeled off when we got to his street. "Laters," he said.

"I know kung fu!" I shouted.

Rubin cracked up.

Darci tilted her head. "You don't know kung fu, Calvin."

"Just kidding, Darce. It's a joke."

Back home on our street, Maya and Willy waved and headed to their houses, which were next door to each other.

When we got to Julio's, I stopped and cocked my ear.

Something was in the air. A sound. Distant, but growing louder.

Boooom. Boooom. Boooom.

"Clarence," I said.

Seconds later, a big pink car with a black stripe down the middle turned onto our street.

"Stella's ride," Julio said.

Boooom. Boooom.

We watched as Clarence's old-time car cruised by in slow motion, gangster music blasting. Stella sat close to Clarence in the front seat.

Clarence glanced over and nodded. Stella ignored us.

"Put your junk away," I said to Julio. "Come to my house."

"Why? We got homework."

"Later. You don't want to miss this."

"Miss what?"

I leaned close. "Stella. She's getting her driver's license. Clarence is teaching her how to drive."

"So?"

"So she's a—"

"Bad driver," Darci said.

I nodded. "Worse. More like *scary*. Come watch. She might practice."

Julio grinned. "Be right back."

Darci and I waited.

Down at the end of the street, Clarence pulled into our driveway. The booming radio went off.

Clarence got out of the car. He was almost as tall as Mom's boyfriend, Ledward, who was six foot seven. I liked Clarence. He was not only teaching Stella how to drive, he was also teaching Darci and Willy how to swim better.

Julio's screen door slapped shut behind us. "Let's go get a front-row seat."

Back at my house, Streak leaped all over me as Julio and I headed through the garage toward the kitchen door. "Hang on, girl. I'll be right back out."

Julio waited in the garage with Streak. Stella made Julio nervous, unless Mom was home. But Mom was still at work.

Darci and I went in the house.

Clarence was sitting at the kitchen counter reading Stella's driver's manual.

Darci and I dropped our backpacks on the floor.

Clarence looked up and lifted his chin, Hey.

"Are you taking Stella out to practice again?" I asked.

"Yep."

"Now?"

"Soon as she comes back out."

"What's she doing?"

"Changing into her driving clothes."

I studied him. "Driving clothes?"

Clarence chuckled.

Darci and I went back outside and plopped down next to Julio and Streak. We didn't have to wait long.

Stella's driving clothes were a light blue shirt, white shorts, and running shoes. She glanced at us, the bright sun making her long hair shine like gold. "What are you doing?" she said.

I shrugged. "Hanging out."

Darci couldn't hold it back. "We want to watch you drive."

Stella shook her head. "No. You can't. Go find something else to do. You'll make me nervous."

Darci and Julio started to get up.

But I didn't move. Good that she was nervous. I owed her for making me shrink.

I leaned back on my hands and smiled.

Stella made a fist and ground it into her palm. "You want some of this, Stump? You want some Texas Nice?"

Stella had come to live with us from Texas. She said they didn't put up with fools like me there. Fools got Texas Nice, every time.

Me and Darci hadn't seen what Texas Nice was yet, but whatever it was, I didn't think Stella would show us with Clarence around.

"Go ahead," I said.

Stella murdered me with her eyes, then huffed and slipped behind the steering wheel of Clarence's big pink car.

Clarence went around to the other side and ducked into the passenger seat.

Stella started the car and gunned the engine.

Varrrooooom!

Julio and Darci took a step back.

Stella glanced in the rearview mirror. A loud squeal came from the tires as she screeched out of the driveway.

4

Circling the Park

Clarence grabbed the dashboard as Stella
bounced to a jolting stop halfway into the
weeds on the other side of the road.

Ho!

Julio and Darci froze.

Streak scurried back into the garage.

Dust rose around the car as it sat there

idling. Stella looked grim, her hands gripping the wheel.

I jumped up and down. "Yee-haw!"

The car jerked forward. A foot. Another foot.

Then the engine died. Stella covered her face with her hands.

"I told you this would be good!" I shouted to Julio. "I told you!"

Julio was still speechless.

Clarence blinked and reached over to touch Stella's shoulder. He said something.

Stella nodded and dropped her hands from the steering wheel. She looked over at us.

I covered my mouth and pointed at her, making like I was laughing.

"Don't," Julio said, grabbing my arm. "She might make that guy come get us."

"I know kung fu," I said.

Stella started the car.

Clarence motioned for her to head slowly up the street. He hung on to the dashboard with one hand.

Stella jerked the car forward and got it going smoothly. She drove up the street about as fast as I could walk. Julio, Darci, and I followed them. Streak came out of the garage and trailed us, too, but kept her distance.

"I can't believe Clarence lets her drive his car," I said.

Clarence loved his car. He was always inspecting it for scratches and nicks. He even carried rags in his trunk to wipe dust off the paint. The car was a classic.

So why would he let Stella even *touch* it?

Stella picked up speed.

We started jogging to keep up. Streak was feeling braver now, running ahead, barking.

Up the street, Willy and Maya were tossing a Frisbee around. Stella and Clarence headed toward them. Willy and Maya moved to the side of the road, and Stella drove past without hitting them.

"What's going on?" Willy asked when we ran up.

"Clarence is teaching Stella how to drive," I said. "She drove into the weeds down by my house. Come on. We're following them."

We jogged after the pink car, keeping up as it drifted from one side of the road to the other. Streak backed off.

"Stella's not too good yet, is she?" Maya said.

"Clarence is going to kill her if she hits anything," I said. "Even if she just scratches the paint."

Stella must have been feeling pretty confident, because when we got up by the park, she was going fast enough to get a ticket.

We slowed to a walk, breathing hard.

Julio stopped. "We're getting too close to Tito's house. I hope he's not home."

We all knew not to go any closer, so we headed into the park, watching out for the pokey burrs that stabbed into our feet. The park had a rusty swing set and a metal slide.

"Throw me that Frisbee," Julio said, running out into the field.

We all made a big circle and tossed it back and forth, except for Darci, who went for the swings. Streak tried to steal the Frisbee a few times and finally got it. It took all four of us to get it back.

A few minutes later, Stella and Clarence cruised back down the street on the other side of the park. Stella was driving like a real driver, except she was going too fast. When she got to the stop sign, she stopped with a jolt. Then she put on the blinker, turned the corner, and zoomed around the park again.

Clarence nodded at us as if everything was just fine.

"Man," Julio said, watching Stella speed past. "She got a lead foot. If that was my car I'd be chewing my fingernails."

I humphed. "Was me, I'd hide the key."

Stella and Clarence sped by three more times before heading home.

We started to run after them but quickly slid to a stop.

Tito was sitting with his friends Bozo and Frankie Diamond in somebody's yard between us and our street.

And all three of them were looking right at us.

5

Lizards in the Sun

Tito was grinning his what-can-I-do-to-these-punks grin.

I looked for a way out.

There wasn't any. "What should we do?"

Julio frowned. Meeting up with Tito was never fun. "Go knock on doors until somebody lets us hide in their house?"

Willy laughed.

"I don't get it," Maya said. "How can you be afraid of a doofus like him? Come on, guys, do like what Mr. Purdy always says—soldier up. Tito's not that smart."

"It's not his brain that worries me," I said.

"Follow me. I'll protect you." Maya grabbed Darci's hand and headed down the street.

"This should be interesting," Julio mumbled.

"I know kung fu," I said, only this time no one laughed. I snapped my fingers for Streak to follow me.

Tito, Bozo, and Frankie Diamond were sprawled on the grass like cats in the sun. Tito was still grinning.

Bozo gave us his most criminal stink eye.

Frankie Diamond, like always, just looked amused. I didn't get that guy. He was calm and cool; his hair was always perfectly combed; he wore a nice shiny silver chain around his neck. Sometimes he was friendly. Not like Tito at all. Still, they liked each other.

We tried to pass by like nothing was up.

"Heyyy," Tito said, smiling even bigger when we got close. "It's the Coco-dork gang. Whatchoo punks doing in my neighborhood?"

Maya and Darci kept walking and didn't even glance at him.

"Hey, tough girl," Tito called. "Be nice. Tito might ax you out someday. You might be my girlfrien' . . . when you old enough."

Maya turned, stuck her finger down her throat, and pretended to gag. Gak!

Frankie Diamond threw back his head and laughed.

Tito grinned. "You never know, ah?"

Maya and Darci kept on going.

But when we tried to pass, Tito put up his hand.

We stopped, even though he was lying on the grass and

we were out on the street. We could have run for it.

But we weren't stupid.

Tito hooked his finger at us. "Come, punks. Talk to Tito. I'm bored."

Maya turned and walked backwards. "He's not bored. He's nobody. Don't listen to him."

Tito liked that. "Hey, girl," he said. "When this nobody talks, *everybody* listens." He grinned at us. "Ain't that right, little punks?"

Julio, Willy, and I nodded. Yeah, sure, Tito, whatever. It was either that or get beat up at school.

Tito tapped the grass with his hand. "Come. Sit."

We sat.

Maya and Darci left us to our fate.

Tito pointed his chin toward Streak, who lay on the grass next to me, panting. "What kind dog that? Chihuahua, or what?"

I shrugged. "Just a mutt."

"Tito," Bozo said. "Ax um if it bites."

Tito looked at me. "Well?"

"She won't bite."

"She? How come you didn't get a boy dog? Only girls get girl dogs."

I shrugged. "I like this one."

Frankie Diamond made kissing sounds and snapped his fingers for Streak to come to him.

Frankie was sitting cross-legged, and Streak jumped into his lap. He scratched her chin.

Tito yawned and stretched. He kicked me,

not hard, just enough to get my attention. "Who's that goofball in your class, wears those black boots? Where he came from?"

"He just moved here from Hilo."

Tito nodded. "Hilo. Never been there." He thought a moment. "What's with those glasses? He like be one cop, or what?"

"He's weird," Julio said.

Willy nodded. "Different."

Tito stared at Willy. "You diff'rent, too, haole boy. You know that, right?"

Willy looked away. He knew that *haole boy* meant *white boy.* "Uh . . . yeah. I guess."

"Whatchoo mean, you guess?" Bozo spat. "If Tito say you diff'rent, you diff'rent."

"Leave him alone," I snapped.

Bozo popped up. "What?"

Ooops.

Tito raised his hand. "S'okay, Bozo. I got it."

Bozo sat back down slowly, his cold gaze burning into me.

Frankie Diamond just sat there scratching Streak's chin, her eyes closed. Happy dog.

Tito looked at me. "So, the boy-cop got a name?"

"Benny Obi."

Tito nodded. "Can he fight?"

"What?"

"I said, is he a fighter like me or a sissy like you?"

If just for five minutes I could be the Incredible Hulk. Ho, man, would I have some fun.

"He knows kung fu," I said.

Tito smiled, his teeth bright white in the sun. "Ahhh, kung fu . . . good, good. Kung fu is good."

Bozo humphed. "You know kung fu, too, ah, Tito?"

Tito spat on the grass. "I know something better. It's called I-broke-your-face fu."

Bozo fell back on the grass laughing.

Tito turned to me again. "We going see whose fu is better, ah?"

6

Obake

"Weird stuff went on around my house in Hilo," Benny Obi told us the next day.

Julio, Rubin, Willy, Maya, and I were sitting on the grass at recess, like always. This time, Benny had come, too. He stood looking down on us wearing his shiny police glasses.

We squinted up at him.

"Ghosts or spirits or night marchers or something, I don't know because I never actually saw them, but for sure they weren't people, because people couldn't do what they did without heavy machinery. . . . I say *they*, but it could have been an *it* . . . I don't know . . . I mean, how can you tell?"

Huh?

"What are you talking about?" Julio said. "Make sense."

Benny Obi tapped a finger on his chin. "I wonder if it was an it. Huh. I tell you anyways. . . . See, we lived outside of town, and all around us was like ranch land with cows and wild pigs and all that, and there was this dirt road by my house that ran up into the country above our place, and one day I woke up and looked out the window and there it was, in the middle of the road, right by my house . . . a giant boulder."

He looked at us, letting his words sink in.

"Was *big*, I tell you, too big for one or two

or even five guys to put there, like the size of a refrigerator." Benny shook his head. "Must have weighed a ton."

Julio smirked and whispered, "Freaky deaky."

If Benny heard, he was unfazed. "Maybe a bulldozer could put it there," he went on. "Or a front-end loader, if it was a big one. But nobody ever heard any heavy machinery like that in the night, so how did that giant rock get there?"

"*Obake,*" Rubin said. "Ghosts. Only way."

Benny pointed at Rubin. "You got it. *Obake.*"

Julio looked at Rubin like, Are you serious? You really believe this stuff?

Rubin frowned. "Well, how else would you explain it?"

"So what happened?" Willy asked. "Did you just leave it in the road?"

"My dad got some of his friends. One of them worked for the county, and he drove up a county front-end loader and pushed the boulder to the side of the road. He was real nervous doing it, too, because he believed it was ghosts who put it there and he didn't want the ghosts to get mad and come to his house and do something weird."

Rubin's eyes got big. "Like what?"

"Like put a skeleton in his kitchen, because he heard *obake* do that sometimes."

"They do?"

"Yeah, for real, they sit a skeleton in a chair like it's eating breakfast and then you wake up and find it at your table. Man, that would *freak . . . me . . . out!*"

Maya yelped out a laugh.

Benny looked at her and wagged his finger. "You should show respect for what you don't know, or else *obake* might come to your house, too."

"You know what?" Maya said, getting up. "I just remembered I was supposed to hang out with normal people."

Maya left just as Tito, Bozo, and Frankie Diamond walked by.

"Hey, tough girl," Tito said. "Last night I saw you in my dream."

Maya turned to walk backwards. "Yeah? I saw you in my nightmare."

Frankie Diamond nearly fell over laughing.

Tito grinned. "She pretty quick."

"Lucky she's a girl," Bozo mumbled.

When Tito noticed Benny Obi, he stopped and stared. Seconds ticked by.

I held my breath.

Finally, Tito turned, spat, and walked on.

"Ho," I whispered.

"I hate when he does that," Julio said. "You can't tell if he going jump you, or what."

Benny Obi went on as if nothing had happened. "Like I was saying, my dad and his friends pushed that boulder off the road into the weeds, and that night when I tried to sleep I couldn't because I kept listening for noises outside . . . but then I fell asleep sometime around three o'clock, and when I woke up the next morning I ran outside to look at the road . . . and there it was . . . again!"

He shook his head, then pulled off his dark glasses, cleaned them on his T-shirt, and put them back on.

"Holy moley," Rubin said.

Benny nodded. "*Obake.* Only answer."

Willy's mouth hung open.

I wanted to ask Benny Obi if the boulder was still in the road when he moved away, but I was too spooked. Already I might get nightmares. I heard stories of weird stuff like that all the time. Ledward was full of them. Clarence, too, if you got him going.

Benny looked over to where Tito, Bozo, and Frankie Diamond were sitting in the shade of a monkeypod tree. "Who are those guys?"

"Stay away from them," I said.

"Why?"

"They're trouble, that's why," Julio said. "That one guy, Tito—the one who stared at you—he could ruin your day, if he wanted."

Benny studied Tito a moment longer. "I'm not scared of him."

Willy shivered. "You should be."

"Really," I said. "He's not your friend. He's mean."

"Tito knows kung fu, too, I bet," Julio added.

"So?" Benny said, keeping his eyes on Tito.

Julio shrugged. "Just saying."

7

A Clean Car

When Darci and I got home after school, we found Clarence in our driveway, washing his car with a fat sponge and a bucket of soapy water. The garden hose gurgled water by his feet.

"How come you're doing that?" I asked. "It wasn't even dirty. It's never dirty."

"That's because I keep it clean." Clarence squirted soap off the hood, then went over and turned off the spigot.

He came back and crouched down to run his finger over a scratch on the front fender. It was so small Darci and I had to move up close to see it. "Did Stella do that?" I asked.

Clarence nodded. "I going fix it now. Like see some magic?"

"Sure," I said, crouching down next to him. Clarence was big, like Ledward.

Darci shook her head and went into the house.

Clarence gave me a grin. "Man stuff, ah?"

"Man stuff."

I followed Clarence to the back of the car. He opened the trunk. Inside, it was as clean and neat as Frankie Diamond's haircut. Not a thing out of place.

Clarence looked in a cardboard box and pulled out a can. He held it up. "Scratch remover."

"I thought you had to paint over scratches."

He grabbed a rag from the box. "Only the big ones."

We crouched around the scratch.

"How did you even see it?" I asked. "It's so small."

Clarence chuckled. "I notice everything. Watch this."

He opened the can, dabbed some of the scratch remover on the rag, and rubbed it across the scratch. We watched the spot turn white in the sun. When it was dry, Clarence rubbed it off.

Poof. The scratch was gone.

"Wow," I said.

"Someday when you get your own car, keep it clean. Nothing like a clean car. And when you get some kind of problem with it, fix it. Right away. Don't wait for um to get more worse. Take care of your car and it will treat you right."

Uh . . . okay.

Clarence put the scratch remover and the rag back in the trunk. The screen door slapped open and Stella came out of the house.

She glared at me. "What are *you* doing here?"

"I live here."

"You know what I mean."

"I'm talking to Clarence."

"About what?" She glanced at Clarence, then back at me. "My driving?"

Clarence put up his hands in surrender.

"We weren't, but we can," I said. "Where should we start?"

Stella bent down so we were nose to nose. "How about right here, Stump?"

Never fight with a skunk, Ledward once told me. Even if you win you still come out smelling bad. I stepped back.

Stella poked me with her finger. "Smart move, Shrimp."

"Watch it," I said. "I know kung fu."

"What?"

"Oh, sorry. For you it would be kung fooey." I grinned and headed into the house.

One good thing about me is I get over stuff quick.

Except for stuff like skulls in lava tubes, and getting eaten by rats, and *obake* who put boulders in your road. That kind of stuff gives me nightmares.

And that night, thanks to Benny Obi, I had nightmares.

The next morning my sheets were twisted around my legs. My pillow was on the floor and Streak was sleeping on it. I peeked over at my clock. Only 5:48. I rolled onto my side and looked out the window. No boulders in the driveway or out on the street.

Dang Benny. He was so weird.

And he got weirder.

8

Bugs

As usual, I walked to school with Darci, Julio, and Willy. Maya rode ahead on her skate-board. Some days she rode it slowly so we could keep up with her. But this day she wanted speed.

"Just think," Julio said, slapping my back as

we walked. "In a few weeks Stella can drive you to school."

I nearly choked. This could actually be true! "But . . . but . . . she doesn't have a car."

Julio grinned. "Yet."

The thought of being in a car with Stella at the wheel made me cringe. I could see us getting from our house to school in about three minutes, garbage cans and mailboxes lying in the streets behind us.

The second we walked into the schoolyard, Willy tapped my arm. "Check it out. Something's going on."

A pack of kids were bunched up over by the cafeteria. The kids in back were jumping to see over the ones in front. Looked like the entire fourth grade was there.

"Let's go!" I said.

We all ran over, except for Darci, who headed to her classroom.

"Ahhh!" somebody gasped.

"Eeew!"

"Gross!"

Willy, Julio, and I pushed and shoved our way to the front. Facing us . . . was Benny Obi.

"What's going on?" I asked Ace, who sat a couple rows behind me in Mr. Purdy's class.

"Benny's eating bugs."

"What?"

"Sick," Julio said, his eyes bulging.

When Benny saw us, he held up a box about the size of a deck of cards. The label on it read LARVETS. "Dried worms," he said.

Ick.

Benny grinned and read the print on the box. "'Real edible worms! Original snacks in barbecue sauce, cheddar cheese, and Mexican spice. Flavored for your eating pleasure. Savor the crunch!'"

Savor the crunch? Gotta be kidding.

He took one out. It looked like a small French fry.

But it was a worm. Dried-out and stiff.

Benny put it in his mouth and made it crunch loud enough for everyone to hear.

"Aww, man!" someone said.

Someone else made a gakking sound.

"You're going to get sick, new kid!"

"That's so gross!"

Benny crunched louder, then swallowed and smacked his lips. Man, he was as weird as a caged mongoose.

"Got something else, too," he said. "Check it out."

He put the box of Larvets in his baggy pants pocket and took out another one. "Crick-Ettes," he said, and read the label. "'Real edible crickets! Original snacks in salt and vinegar, bacon and cheddar cheese, and sour cream and onion seasoning.' Yum!"

Maya squeezed in next to us. "What's going on?"

"Benny's eating bugs."

"Serious?"

"Worms and crickets . . . so far."

Benny held up a dried cricket for Maya to see. "Tasty treats," he said, and dropped it in his mouth.

Crunch.

Maya stared at him. "You know what, Benny? There's something wrong with you. Seriously. People don't eat bugs."

"What do you mean?" Benny said, sticking his fingers into the box for another cricket. "People eat bugs all over the world. Bugs have nutrients. Here, try one."

He held out a cricket to Maya.

Maya jumped back. The cricket looked like some dead old dried-up bug you'd find under your bed or in your closet. "Get that out of my face!"

Benny tossed it into his mouth.

Snap! Crunch!

I nudged Julio with my elbow. "All day sitting next to him, you're going to smell bug breath."

Julio scowled. "If I do, I'll . . . I'll . . ."

I cracked up.

"Shuddup."

I laughed harder.

The bell rang and the crowd broke up.

Benny stuffed the box of Crick-Ettes back into his baggy pants and patted his pocket.

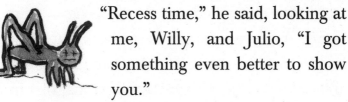

"Recess time," he said, looking at me, Willy, and Julio, "I got something even better to show you."

"Can't wait," Julio mumbled.

All morning Mr. Purdy went on about some old civilization in Mexico. But I was only half listening because I was in the front row. Which meant I was close to Mr. Purdy's desk. And on Mr. Purdy's desk was our class pet, Manly Stanley, the centipede—a bug.

"Watch your back, Manly," I whispered. "Benny's eating bugs today."

Manly looked up. Huh?

"Mr. Coconut?"

"Uh . . . yeah?"

Mr. Purdy gave me the pay-attention-or-die teacher look. "Am I boring you this morning?"

"Ah, no, Mr. Purdy. I'm listening."

"Huh," Mr. Purdy said. "Could have fooled me."

"You were talking about . . . Mexico?"

Mr. Purdy studied me, shook his head, then turned back to the class. Lucky I at least caught that one word. The day had just started and already Benny Obi was getting me in trouble.

After lunch, all the guys in our class went out on the field with Benny. He had more stuff in his baggy pants pockets.

The girls stayed away. Benny's bugs were too gross for them.

"Check this out," Benny said as we crowded around him.

He looked up over our heads, like he was

making sure no teachers were around. I looked up, too. Was he going to do something that might *really* get us into trouble?

Benny pulled another small box out of his deep-pocket pants. He kept the label covered so we couldn't see it.

Man, he had a whole grocery store in those pants.

Benny grinned. "The star of them all."

"Show us."

"What is it?"

"Come on, new kid."

Still keeping the label covered, Benny opened the box and pulled out another kind of bug. He held it up, admiring it. "Chocolate-covered."

"What is it?" Willy asked.

"What does it look like?"

We inched closer. Its tail was curved. "No," I gasped. "A scorpion?"

Everyone stepped back.

Benny laughed. "It's dead. Don't worry."

"Holy bazooks!" someone cried. The bug

had pokey horns and a curved tail, all covered in chocolate.

"Is there *really* a scorpion in there?" I asked. "Or is it just chocolate shaped like one?"

"It's real," Benny said. "Watch."

He held it up by its stinger tail and lowered it halfway into his mouth.

I held my breath. Nobody but *nobody* eats scorpions, I don't care how many nutrients are in them. There's poison in their stingers.

Snip.

Benny bit it in half, chewed and swallowed, then showed us the half he didn't eat.

"Aw, man," Julio said, putting a hand to his throat.

Because once it was cut in half, you could see the scorpion's dried guts. My stomach rolled. Benny was bat-brain crazy.

He finished off the other half, stuck the box back in his pocket, and pulled out one last thing.

He held it up. "Anyone want it?"

It looked like a lollipop. It had black specks in it.

Julio squinted. "What's in it? Pepper?"

"Ants."

Julio walked away, shaking his head. "I'm outta here."

"I want it," I said, snapping the lollipop out of Benny's hand. I read the label on the clear plastic wrapper. "'Antlix Lollipop.' Cool."

I stuck it in my pocket.

"I saw your dad in Las Vegas," Benny said as the crowd broke up.

I froze. "What? What did you say?"

"Your dad. I saw his show in Las Vegas."

My mind jumped all over the place. No one had ever said anything like that to me before. "No you didn't, Benny. You're making that up. Somebody just told you about him."

My dad *was* in Las Vegas, but still . . .

Benny shrugged. "Think what you want."

"I will," I said.

What a liar. How could he say that to somebody whose dad left them?

Just wasn't right.

Benny headed back toward the classroom.

I scowled at him. He was so full of made-up stuff he couldn't even tell the truth about one thing. Dumb weird weirdo.

As Benny passed the tree where Tito, Bozo, and Frankie Diamond were lounging, Tito picked up a pebble and threw it at him.

The pebble hit Benny in the back.

"Hey, Kung Fu! Come back here! You and me can do some Jackie Chan!"

Benny kept on walking.

"Buuuk-buk-buk," Tito cackled, flapping chicken-wing arms.

9

Student Parking

Back home after school, Darci, Willy, Maya, Julio, and I ran over to Foodland. Clarence was teaching Stella how to park in the parking lot. We wanted a good seat so we scrambled up to sit on the cinder-block wall.

"They'll be here any minute," I said.

Foodland's parking lot was about half full. There were lots of spaces Stella could pull into, and some were the kind you had to back into.

"So what did Benny do after lunch?" Maya asked.

Julio snorted. "Ate a scorpion."

Maya's jaw dropped. "You're kidding."

"Nope. We saw it."

"That's just sick."

Willy elbowed me. "Here they come."

Clarence's big, clean pink-and-black car bounced into the parking lot a little too fast. Stella was driving. Clarence sat in the passenger seat looking calm. How could he do that? Wasn't he worried about his car?

When Stella saw us sitting on the wall she hit the brakes. The car jerked to a stop. She stuck her head out the window. "What are you doing here? Go home! I don't want you watching me."

"Free country," I said.

Stella narrowed her eyes. For sure, I was going to pay for this. But I thought, You know what? It'll be worth it. "Go ahead," I said. "Don't let us stop you."

Clarence sat waiting. He didn't frown or smile or say a word. He was patient, that guy. Nothing seemed to bother him.

Someone pulled into the lot behind them. Stella jerked the car ahead, scowling.

"Hoo-ie," Julio said, slapping his thigh. "You better lock your bedroom door tonight, because she might come in there and tie your neck in a knot."

"I know kung fu," I said.

Julio laughed.

"I can't wait to drive," Willy said. "In

California, my dad let me sit on his lap and steer the car. It was awesome."

"Yeah?"

"I was in second grade the first time I did it."

"Watch," Maya said, nodding toward the parking lot. She pulled a bag of peanut M&M's out of her pocket and passed it around. "Here we go."

Stella was creeping into a parking space between two cars, but Clarence made her stop because the door on his side was about to hit the back bumper of the parked car. Stella backed up and tried again. I noticed Clarence wasn't looking so calm now.

This time Stella did it right. Almost. She'd parked without hitting the cars on either side of her. But if Clarence wanted to get out he'd have to crawl over to Stella's side.

Clarence wiped his forehead with his fingers.

Stella backed out of the parking space, with Clarence sticking his head out the window to watch how close she was coming to the car on his side. Looked like inches to me.

"Lucky no cars are behind her," Willy said. "They'd be honking, she's so slow."

After Stella managed to get the car out of that space, she drove around looking for another one. At the top of the gently sloping parking lot, somebody had left a shopping cart.

Stella hit it.

She jerked to a stop, the bumper tapping the cart and sending it rolling down toward a shiny clean fancy black car.

Clarence jumped out and ran after the runaway cart. He caught it just before it smashed into the black car.

Stella sat gripping the wheel, watching.

Clarence ran the cart over to the cart corral and got back in the car with Stella.

Stella drove around looking for another place to park.

"You know what Benny said yesterday at school?"

Julio turned to me. "Bugs have nutrients?"

"He said he saw my dad in Las Vegas."

Darci leaned forward and looked over at me. "He did? He saw Dad?"

"He's such a liar," I said.

"No kidding," Maya said. "He's like a water faucet on an old house. Whenever you turn it on rust comes out. You can't trust anything he says."

"Yeah," Willy added. "Guy's too weird."

"A freak," Julio said.

I frowned. Calling him a freak didn't feel right. He was just strange, that's all. Different.

"Did it make you feel bad when he said that?" Willy asked.

"Huh . . . what?"

"Did it make you feel bad when Benny said he saw your dad? I mean, lying like that?"

I shrugged. It made me feel something, but I didn't know what.

"Look," Maya said. "She's backing into a parking space."

After six tries, Stella got it right.

Sort of.

10

Antlix

Ledward came over for dinner that night. He brought a key lime pie with graham cracker crust, my all-time favorite dessert in the whole world after coffee ice cream, bread pudding with raisins, and hot fudge sundaes with peanuts.

"How's the driving practice going?" he

asked Stella as we sat at the table eating meat loaf, mashed potatoes and gravy, and boiled soybeans in the pod.

Stella was in one of her don't-bother-me moods.

"Fine," she said, not looking up.

"You got somebody helping you?"

"Yeah."

Ledward nodded. "Who's that?"

"Clarence."

"That big boy with the pink car?"

"Yeah."

"You think you ready for the driving test?"

"Close."

"What's the hardest part?"

"Parking."

I was only half listening, because I was thinking about tasting what I had in my pocket: the Antlix lollipop I got from Benny Obi. Could I actually do it?

"She practiced at Foodland today," Darci told Ledward. "In the parking lot."

"She hit a shopping cart," I added.

Stella glared at me, unblinking.

"Uh . . . but Clarence got out and caught it before it smashed into somebody's car."

The look on Stella's face was turning dangerous.

I studied my plate.

"Stella's a good driver, Led," Mom said. "I've taken her out a couple of times, too. She did just fine."

Ledward nodded and leaned toward Stella. "I know what you can do when you put your mind to it." He reached out and patted Stella's hand.

Stella pulled her hand away.

Ledward tapped the table and sat back.

"We'll all go out to lunch to celebrate when she gets her license," Mom said. "Stella will drive, of course."

"If she passes," I added.

Stella kicked me under the table.

"Ow! What'd you do that for?"

"A bad day is in your future."

"Ooo, I'm scared," I said, reaching down to rub my shin.

Stella grinned. It wasn't pretty.

Then an idea hit me. Oh! Yes!

That's how ideas come; out of no-where. You're just sitting there minding your own business, and *boom*–something good pops up.

"You know what, Stella?" I said. "I take that back. For sure you'll pass. You're not such a bad driver. I mean, over at Foodland you did pretty good."

Stella eyed me.

Mom smiled. "Now, *there* is the Calvin we all know and love."

Dang. I wished she hadn't said that.

Still, this idea was too good to resist.

I turned back to Stella. "Uh . . . because you did so good, me and my friends . . . well, we got you a present."

Stella barked out a laugh. "Ha! Right. And you're still . . . shrinking."

Now I *really* liked my idea.

Darci looked at me and I knew I'd better say something quick before she ruined everything. She'd been with me the whole time and knew we hadn't gotten Stella anything.

I reached into my pocket. "Here," I said, pulling out the Antlix lollipop. "These are really good. They come from . . . from Australia. It's peppermint."

Stella eyed the Antlix. Slowly, she reached across the table and took the lollipop. "What's it got in it? Pepper?"

"That's dried peppermint flakes."

"Peppermint isn't black."

"Australian peppermint is. Try it. You'll see."

Stella peeled off the wrapping, smelled

the lollipop, then licked it. "Doesn't taste at all like peppermint. In fact, it's just sweet . . . like sugar, with no taste."

She licked it again.

I bit my lip, hard. The laugh of a lifetime was about to explode out of me. I could hardly hold it in.

Mom gave me a look that said, Calvin, what are you up to?

Stella studied the lollipop again. "You're lying, as usual. Tell me what those black specks are or I don't want this thing."

I hesitated.

Stretched out the moment.

"Ants."

"What?" Stella held the lollipop closer. Then she grabbed the wrapper and read the label. She shrieked and threw the Antlix at me. I ducked and it hit the wall behind me.

I laughed so hard I fell off my chair.

Stella stood and looked across the table at me. "You're a sick little boy! You need help! You should be in a hospital!"

She stomped down the hall to her room and slammed the door.

Now I was rolling on the floor.

Mom reached over and picked up the label. "Where did you get this, Calvin?"

I was laughing too hard to answer.

Mom looked at Ledward, who sat with a half grin on his face. Like a smart person, he kept his mouth shut.

I tried to pull myself together. "It's a joke, Mom. I got it from a kid at school."

"A joke."

"Yeah . . . just a joke."

Mom didn't say a word for at least a minute.

I picked up my chair and sat back at the table, wiping my eyes.

"Calvin," Mom said. She leaned forward, her elbows on the table. "I want to tell you a little story."

"Okay."

"The reason Stella lives with us is that she and her mom don't get along. Her mom was my best friend in high school before she got married and moved to Texas. You know this, right?"

"Yeah. I think so."

"Well, one day Twyla got angry at Stella. Very angry, and she said something she regrets to this day."

I perked up. "What did she say?"

"She told Stella she was too stupid to ever do anything right."

I held my breath. Stella's mom said that? Really?

"Of course her mother didn't mean it.

But it came out and that was that. The damage was done. Stella stopped speaking to her."

Ledward shook his head.

Darci was silent.

"Let me ask you this," Mom went on, looking into my eyes. "Do you think that being successful at getting a driver's license might mean something to Stella?"

My stomach felt sick.

11

what?

The next day at school I didn't feel much better. Why was I always doing dumb stuff? Was there something wrong with me?

Probably I would have felt bad all day long if Benny hadn't shown up doing dumber things than me.

"Bug man is a very, very, *very* strange dude," Julio said just before school started.

"What's he doing now?"

"Having a one-word day."

"A what?"

Later, at recess, we were sitting on the grass in the shade of a monkeypod tree—Julio, Willy, Rubin, Benny Obi, and me. Benny had attached himself to us whether we wanted him to or not.

Julio leaned close and whispered, "Watch this."

He let a few seconds pass: nice day, nothing going on.

Then: "Hey, Benny, that was funny what you did yesterday. I mean, eating bugs and all."

"What?"

"Where did you get them, anyway?"

"What?"

"Did they taste good?"

"What?"

Rubin and Willy burst out laughing.

I looked at Benny.

Benny grinned.

"See?" Julio said. "A one-word day."

I grinned back. Where did he come up with this stuff?

Julio lay back on the grass and covered his face with his hands. "He's going to drive me crazy."

"Hey, stupits," somebody said.

Julio sat back up.

Tito, Bozo, and Frankie Diamond stood over us.

I reached into my pocket and was relieved to discover that I was broke. Tito had a habit of borrowing your money. Permanently.

Tito crouched by Benny, one knee cocked forward. "Hey, Kung Fu, I heard you eat bugs."

"What?"

Tito squinted. "I heard you eat bugs, I said. Is that right? You eat bugs?"

"What?"

Tito stood.

Oh, man. Benny had no idea who he was messing with.

"Benny," I whispered. "Not now."

Benny looked at me. Luckily he didn't say *what*.

Bozo and Frankie Diamond gave us looks that said trouble was coming. Soon.

Tito squatted back down, his face inches from Benny's. "You disrespecting me, punk? That what you doing?"

Benny hesitated. "What?"

I cringed.

Tito stared at Benny. "Get up," he whispered.

Benny thought about it and, lucky for all of us, got up.

Tito was taller. He looked down on Benny. "I don't like you."

Tito shoved Benny, not hard, but enough to make Benny stagger. "We go, punk. Shake it up. You and me. Right now."

"What?"

Ho!

I scrambled up with Julio, Willy, and Rubin. We backed away.

Tito swung, but Benny ducked and Tito missed.

Tito's face turned red. He started to move toward Benny.

Benny took a stance, anchoring his feet. "I know kung fu," he said, ending his one-word day. "I can't fight you. I could hurt you."

Whoa!

Tito blinked, then snorted. "I got something better. It's called kung-you-dead fu."

Tito moved in, shoving Benny.

Benny staggered back, planted his foot, and charged, his arms wheeling like a loose propeller . . . hitting nothing.

Tito laughed and slapped Benny's arms away.

Benny Obi didn't know how to fight. He didn't know boxing, wrestling, or regular old street-shoving, and he sure didn't know a lick of kung fu.

Zero.

Tito laughed, dancing away from every

one of Benny's useless
windmill swings. "What
a sissy. You don't know
kung fu, what you
know is kung fu-fu.
That's what I going call you.
From now on you going be
Kung Fu-Fu." Tito whooped.
"Fu-Fu, Fu-Fu, Fu-Fu."

"Stop!" someone shouted.

Tito turned.

Benny ran off, heading toward the library.

Maya came up and shoved Tito. She was
even shorter than Benny Obi. "Why are you
always picking on people smaller than you?
Does it make you feel big?"

Aiy, Maya. What are you *doing*?

Tito raised his hands, grinning. "Ho, look.
The girl more brave than Kung Fu-Fu."

"Tito," Frankie Diamond whispered.
"Teacher coming."

I looked behind me. Mr. Tanaka, the

school librarian, was heading toward us.

Tito, still grinning, backed away. He pointed at Maya as if to say, We can talk about this later. He turned and followed his idiot friends toward the tree they'd staked out as their own.

Mr. Tanaka walked up. "We have a problem here?"

We all shook our heads.

Maya scowled at us but said nothing.

Mr. Tanaka crossed his arms and looked over at Tito, Bozo, and Frankie Diamond. "Ohhh-kay," he said, and strolled away.

"Ho, man," I mumbled.

"What?" Julio said.

"I said, ho, man."

"What?"

12

Space Cushion

On Saturday morning, I woke up to the sound of someone talking outside my window. I rolled over to look out.

Stella?

I rubbed my eyes and popped up on my elbows. Stella had a booklet in her hand. Who was she talking to? I couldn't see anyone else.

"Residential neighborhood, twenty-five. School zone, twenty. Driver on the left has the right of way. Never–"

"What are you doing?" I said through the screen. "Who you talking to?"

Stella turned to look at my window, then moved out into the street. Now all I could hear was mumbling.

I slipped off my bunk.

Streak was sleeping on the floor. "Rise and shine, you lazy dog. Go out and pee."

She slapped her tail on the floor but made no move to get up.

"It's your bladder," I said, and went into the house. Mom, who sold jewelry at Macy's in Honolulu, had already left for work. But Darci was finishing up a toasted bagel in the kitchen.

"What's with Stella?" I asked. "She's outside talking to herself."

"She's practicing."

"For what?"

"Did you forget? She's getting her driver's license today. Clarence is taking her."

Right! Driving test day.

Darci brushed the crumbs off her hands. "I'm going to Reena's house."

She left.

I gulped down a bowl of cereal and peeked in on Streak to see if she was ready to get up.

Nope. "You're worse than Julio, you know that?"

Streak looked up at me and slapped her tail on the floor.

I nudged her with my foot. "Come on, Streak. I can't just leave you inside." I wanted to go outside to see what Stella was doing.

Streak stretched and followed me out of the garage.

No Stella. Where was—

"What the—"

Stella was sitting in my rowboat, which was pulled up into the swamp grass down by the water. She held the booklet loosely over the side and stared out at the slow-moving river.

I followed Streak down the sloping yard.

"You can sit in my boat," I said. "No problem. I'll let you."

Stella turned and studied me. "What do you want?"

"What's that booklet?"

"Driver's manual. What's it to you?"

"But you took that test a long time ago."

"I'm taking another one."

"The driving one."

"See? You do have a brain. Sometimes."

I let that go. I was still feeling bad about the Antlix, and what Stella's mom had said to her. That was so . . . mean.

I squatted to pet Streak. "Uh . . . you want me to quiz you?"

When Stella didn't answer, I stood. "Guess not." I turned to head back up to the house.

"Here," she said, waving the booklet in my direction. "Just pick stuff at random."

Everything I asked her she got right, except for one thing.

"Here's a weird one," I said. "What's a space cushion?"

Stella eyed me. "Is that really in there or are you making it up?"

"No, it's in here. Look." I started to show her.

She held up a hand. "Wait . . . it's really in there?"

I tapped the page. "Right here."

She frowned. "I can't believe I don't remember it. I've read that manual five times, cover to cover." She closed her eyes, trying to remember. "Oh, just tell me," she finally said. "My mind's a blank."

"All you have to do to remember is think of Tito."

"Who?"

She didn't remember Tito, who'd once called her *Stel-la* and said he liked older women. Never mind. "Okay, listen. Is there anyone you don't like, like maybe someone at school?"

"What does that have to do with what we were talking about?"

"Well, is there?"

She thought. "Okay, there's these three girls. I don't know them, and I'm not sure I want to. They give me the creeps."

"So what do you do when you see them?"

"Stay away from them. So, listen, if you don't want to quiz me just give that booklet back."

"There you go," I said. "That's how you remember what a space cushion is. Stay away. Keep your distance. Give yourself some space. This is what it says."

I flipped to the page and read aloud.

"'When a driver makes a mistake, other drivers need time to react. The only way you can be sure you have enough time to react is by leaving plenty of space between your vehicle and the vehicles around you. That space becomes a 'space cushion.'"

I looked up. "See?"

Stella grinned. "You remember that yourself, Stump . . . next time you give me a lollipop with ants in it."

"Uh–"

Saved by the blast of a car horn.

"Clarence!" Stella scrambled out of the skiff.

We both ran up the yard toward the house.

Clarence was waiting in the car, his arm hanging out the open window. "You ready?"

"As I'll ever be," Stella said. "Let's go."

"Hey, your booklet." I held it up.

"Keep it. Maybe when you're fifty they'll let you drive."

"Hardy-har."

Clarence flicked his eyebrows at me, Hey.

I lifted my chin.

Before Stella got in the car she glanced back at me. "Space cushion. I'll never forget it. Thanks."

"Yeah . . . and sorry about the ants."

"That's okay, Stump. It wasn't that much of a surprise."

"It wasn't?"

"You expect stuff like that from a moron."

Stella winked and got in the car.

13

weird Stuff

A couple hours later, I was tossing around a football with Willy and Julio when Clarence's big pink car came cruising down the street. Willy and Julio jumped to the side of the road. Stella was driving.

I stayed out in the street.

Stella pulled up next to me and stopped.

We crowded around the window.

"So?" I asked.

Stella flashed her brand-new driver's license and a grin that said, Dang it, I did it!

I took the license. Her picture was pretty good. Better than Mom's. "Someday I'll get one of these, too. Is it hard to drive?"

"If I can do it, you can do it. . . . No, wait . . . that's not right. . . . I forgot you're a moron."

Stella snatched back her license. "But you could probably get a bicycle license."

She drove away with a toot of the horn. Before she got ten feet the radio came on.

Boooom. Boooom. Boooom.

Willy, Julio, and I danced to the beat, grinning like idiots.

We played football in the street until Mom came home. It was starting to get dark by then.

She waved when she drove by.

"Gotta go," I said, and tossed Julio his football.

Julio caught it one-handed. "Me and Willy might watch Stella drive you to school on Monday."

"Want a lift?"

Julio grinned. "Not in this life."

When I got home, Clarence was squatting down by his car, petting Streak.

"What are you doing?" I asked. "Where's Stella?"

"Which one you like me to answer?"

I squatted next to him and scratched Streak's chin. "She's got fleas."

"Who? Stella?"

I laughed. Funny!

"Hey," I said. "Can I ask you a question?"

"Shoot."

"So . . . uh, well . . . you got any, you know, like really weird kids in your class?"

Clarence was a senior at Kailua High School. He was bound to know at least one.

Clarence chuckled. "Couple, three. Why?"

I shrugged. "What does *lead foot* mean? My friend Julio said Stella had one."

"Ho, you have a strange way of asking questions, you know?"

"Sorry."

Clarence stood. "Let's see. Lead foot could be couple things. Your friend prob'ly said that because she drives liddle bit fast, ah?" He grinned. "Heavy foot on the pedal."

"Ah." That made sense. Lead was heavy.

"Also it could mean you dragging your feet. You know, slow, taking your time, not moving fast. You could say you got a lead foot that way, too."

I nodded. That made sense, too.

"Why you asked about weird kids?"

Streak rolled over for me to rub her belly. "Well . . . at my school? We got this new guy. From Hilo. I've never seen anyone like him. I mean, he tells weird stories, eats bugs, has one-word days, and knows kung fu . . . but really doesn't . . . I mean, know kung fu, he just said he did . . . and then he got in a fight and ran away." I frowned and scratched the back of my head. "Now he's got Tito on his back."

"Who's Tito?"

"A sixth grader who likes to push us around."

Clarence thought for a moment. "This Tito messes with you?"

"Sometimes."

"You like me talk to him?"

"No, no, Tito's not that bad. I can handle him. I mean, I know how. But this kid . . ."

I shook my head.

"I knew a kid like that one time," Clarence said. "Not the Tito one, but the other one.

Everything you said, he made it more big. Whatever you did, he did um better. Everything. No way you could top him." Clarence humphed. "He got in a lot of fights."

"Really? This new kid—his name is Benny—he's kind of like that. But maybe half of what he says might be true."

"What I think," Clarence said, "is that guys like that . . . they unsure of themselves. They just trying to figure it out."

"Figure what out?"

Clarence shrugged. "Life, I guess."

I nodded but didn't really understand. "I can't wait to drive."

Clarence chuckled. "You like sit behind the wheel?"

"Ho, yeah! Can I?"

"Get in."

Clarence opened the door of his big pink car and I slipped into the driver's seat. I gripped the steering wheel in both hands. I stretched to see over the hood. "This is a big car."

"How they made these old ones."

No wonder Stella hit stuff in it. You couldn't even see.

Clarence looked toward the house. "Stella told me: go wait by the car, I coming right out. That was ten minutes ago."

I laughed. "Here's a secret: pretend you don't care."

Clarence raised an eyebrow. "How come?"

"Your life will be better."

"Good call."

14

The Nasty R

Benny Obi was prob'ly home figuring out life, because the next day he wasn't at school.

"Settle down, class," Mr. Purdy said as school started. "This morning we're going to take a few minutes to talk about the nasty *R*. It's nasty because we don't want any part of it in our school. Anyone care to guess what it is?"

I was slumping in my chair, the hot morning sun pouring through the open window.

Rubin's hand shot up. "Reading?"

Mr. Purdy stared at Rubin.

"Oh . . . yeah," Rubin said. "We like reading."

Hmmm. What starts with *R* and is nasty? "Rats?" I said.

Mr. Purdy smiled. "We have rats here, Calvin?"

"Uh . . . I don't think so."

"No, we don't have rats. The nasty *R* I'm talking about, class, is ridicule . . . because we have a problem."

That got me sitting up straight.

The room got quiet. Very quiet.

Mr. Purdy folded his arms and studied us. "It seems some people in this school have been giving our newest student a hard time."

Heads turned toward Benny Obi's empty seat.

"Yes," Mr. Purdy said. "He's not here today, is he? Does anyone have an idea why?"

Silence like the bottom of the sea.

"Ridicule," Mr. Purdy went on. "Disrespect. Bullying. Know what those are, class?"

A few mumbles and nods. Shuffling of feet. Staring at hands.

"Something happened on the playground yesterday. We don't know exactly what, but we have an idea who was involved. If anyone cares to talk about it, come see me later. But here's the thing: I know that *my* students—even those of you who might have been there— don't ridicule anyone. We don't disrespect anyone, or tease anyone, or make fun of anyone. We respect and support each other, even if someone is different from us. Isn't that right?"

Everyone nodded.

Mr. Purdy looked us over, every one of us. He didn't look mad, just serious. "Thank you," he said finally. "I'm counting on you. You are much better than what went on yesterday. I know this, because I believe in you and expect you to uphold the standards of Mr.

Purdy's fourth-grade boot camp wherever you are."

Mr. Purdy let that sink in.

After a long moment of silence, Ace raised his hand. "Is Benny coming back, Mr. Purdy?"

"I sure hope so, Ace."

Man, I thought. If I were Benny Obi would I come back? It would be so hard. You'd have to face everyone knowing you'd made a fool of yourself after they'd seen that you didn't know kung fu and had run away.

Ace nodded. "Me too, Mr. Purdy."

At recess, I was sitting in the shade with Julio, Willy, and Rubin.

"I still can't believe he ate bugs," Willy said.

Julio tossed a pebble and searched the dry grass for another one. "He did it to get attention. That's what my dad said."

I looked at Julio. "You told your dad?"

Julio shrugged.

"Did you tell him about Tito, too?"

"Yeah. I felt kind of bad, you know? I mean, sure Benny made the kung fu thing up, but he didn't deserve to be pushed around by some . . . some–"

"Bully," I said.

"I kind of liked Benny," Willy said. "He always had something crazy to say or do. He wasn't boring."

We all nodded.

Then clammed up when three shadows fell over us.

Tito kicked my foot. "Where's Kung Fu-

Fu? I don't see him here today. Me and him's got more business."

I shaded my eyes and looked up. Bozo and Frankie Diamond stood behind him. Tito raised an eyebrow.

"He didn't come to school today," I said.

Tito smirked. "Scared, ah?"

"You didn't have to do what you did to him," Julio said.

Ho, Julio!

Tito glared at Julio. "You like I do it to you, too, punk? 'Cause I can. I make you one sissy-fu, too."

Julio stood.

Tito took a step toward him.

I sprang up and put my hand on Tito's chest. I didn't think. It just happened. "No, Tito."

Tito looked at my hand. "Whatchoo think you're doing?"

Yeah, what?

"If you were me," I said, not moving my

hand, "would you sit here and let someone like you push your friend around?"

Willy got up, too.

Tito's eyes drilled into mine, his face stone cold. Bozo and Frankie Diamond stepped closer.

I'm dead, I thought. Prob'ly Willy and Julio, too.

Tito poked my chest with his finger. "You got guts, Coco-punk. I respect that."

I let my hand drop.

Tito gave me a long look and nodded. The three big guys slouched away, walking and talking tough.

I let out a breath.

"Man, Calvin," Julio said. "Where did *that* come from?"

I held out my hand. "Look at my fingers."

They were trembling like Clarence's idling car.

That night Mom brought home a cherry pie with vanilla ice cream and a postcard. The picture on the postcard was of Kailua Bay. The colors were way brighter than you ever saw them in real life.

She handed the postcard to Stella. "After we celebrate your driver's license victory, send your mom this card and share the news.

I've already stamped and addressed it for you."

Stella took the postcard. She turned it over, studied the front again, then handed it back to Mom. "She doesn't care, so I don't need this."

"Of course she cares!" Mom said.

Stella just looked at her.

"Your mom loves you, Stella. I know that."

Stella frowned and snapped the card out of Mom's hand.

Later, when Mom told me to take the trash out to the garage, I found the postcard in the trash bag.

I stuck it in my pocket.

15

Rock On!

When school started the next day, Benny Obi's desk still sat vacant. Was he scared to come to school because of Tito? Was he embarrassed? Even Julio kept glancing at the door to see if he'd show up.

Mr. Purdy was writing math problems on the whiteboard.

"Where's Benny, Mr. Purdy?" Shayla finally asked. "Have you heard from him?"

Mr. Purdy finished the problem he'd begun, then put the marker on the tray and turned to face us. "I was going to give it another day or two before I said anything," he said with a sigh. "But I don't think it's going to change." He shook his head.

What was he talking about?

"Benny isn't coming back. He's transferred to another school."

What?

A deep hush fell over the classroom.

Mr. Purdy sat on the edge of his desk and looked at us until we started to fidget. "We still don't know why he left. His parents didn't say. But if any of you has an idea, I hope you will consider talking to me about it. Kailua Elementary is a great school, and I personally want to do everything I can to keep it that way."

I still felt squirmy inside. I wanted to tell him what happened. But I didn't, too. If we told him about Tito, and Tito got in trouble, things would get worse. No, there was a better way. Stand by your friends in the first place, and don't let guys like Tito get in their face.

Mr. Purdy took a deep breath and let it out through puffed cheeks. He clapped once. "Take out a clean sheet of paper, boot campers. We have work to do."

When I reached into my desk I got the surprise of my life.

My jaw dropped.

What?

It was a picture. There was a yellow sticky note on it.

He was good. I liked his show.
It was good meeting you, too.
I hope you liked the Antlix.
Laters.

I peeled the sticky note away and studied the man looking back at me in the shiny autographed black-and-white photograph.

Rock on, Benny Obi!
Little Johnny Coconut

16

Another Dumb Idea

When I got home from school I went straight to my bedroom, propped Benny's photo of my dad up on my desk, and sat on my lower bunk staring at it.

Rock on, Benny Obi!

He'd really done it. He'd actually seen

Little Johnny Coconut in Las Vegas. He hadn't lied. He hadn't made it up.

Boy, did I feel small.

Benny Obi, why were you so weird? How did you get that picture in my desk at school? Why did you change schools?

And why did you tell Tito you knew kung fu? That was really dumb, Benny. You should have . . .

No.

We should have stepped up for you.

Streak scratched at my door. I got up to let her in.

"Wassup, dog?"

I flopped back down on my lower bunk. Streak jumped up and lay next to me. I closed my eyes. Benny Obi had given me his special autographed photo. And he'd found a way to sneak it into my desk without anyone seeing him. You don't do stuff like that for just anybody.

I sighed and put my hand on Streak's head. "I messed up, girl."

Streak licked my hand.

I just wanted to lie there. I didn't feel like doing anything.

When I finally opened my eyes I noticed the postcard on my desk, the one Stella had thrown in the trash.

I got up and stood looking down at it.

Kailua Bay never looked so good as it did in that picture on the card. An idea popped into my head.

Could I?

I frowned and searched for a pen.

Just do it.

Dear Mom,

I got my driver's license! I like driving. Mrs. Coconut says I'm pretty good at it. Calvin and Darci think so, too. Well, I just thought you'd like to know. I'm fine. How are you?

Love,

Stella

I had no idea why I wrote that. It just came out. It's like what Mr. Purdy told us about writing a story. Even though you might not know exactly what your story is about, or where it's going, once you start writing, stuff happens. It's magic.

Or dumb.

Now what?

I moved Benny Obi's Little Johnny Coconut photograph next to my own Little Johnny Coconut photograph and stuck the postcard in my back pocket.

As I was heading out of my room, Clarence drove up in his big pink car. Stella was with him.

I went out into the sun.

Clarence lifted his chin, Hey.

I nodded back.

Stella got out with her books. She thunked the car door shut and leaned into the open window. "Thanks for the ride. Call me."

Clarence winked, backed out, and drove off with a short toot of the horn.

Stella and I watched him drive away.

Then she seemed to realize for the first time that I was standing next to her. "Why are *you* here?"

"Why not?"

She squinted. "You're pushing it, Stump."

"Why not?"

Stella banged past me, heading through the garage and into the house. I followed her, catching the door as it was about to slam into my face. "Hey!"

"Sorry," she said in fake surprise. "I didn't see you. Oh, that's why . . . I forgot. You shrunk."

Stella laughed and dropped her books on the kitchen counter.

"Why are you following me around?"

"Why not?"

"This is why not," she said, moving toward me. "I don't like it; it's annoying; you're getting on my nerves. Beat it."

"Fine. But I have something for you."

"And what might that be?" Stella eyed me.

I pulled the postcard out of my back pocket and handed it to her. "You should send this to your mom."

Stella read it.

She held it a long time, just looking at it.

She closed her eyes and shook her head. "Stump . . ."

I waited, nervous about what I'd done.

Stella opened her eyes and held the card up close to my face. She ripped it in half. "Mind your own business."

The postcard, now in two pieces, went back into the trash under the sink.

I bit my lower lip.

Another dumb idea.

17

Like a Rock

Five minutes after me, Willy, and Julio walked into the schoolyard the next day, Tito and his doofy shadows came up and got in my face.

"Where's Kung Fu-Fu? How come I don't see him here? Where he's at, ah? Hiding from me? Crying to his mommy? Tell me, you so brave."

Bozo and Frankie Diamond closed in on the sides.

Julio and Willy stepped back.

"He's gone," I said. "Because of you."

Tito grinned. "You kine of cocky today, ah?"

"You didn't have to embarrass him."

Tito poked my chest with his finger. "Maybe I embarrass you."

Julio and Willy came back and stood beside me.

"You can try," I said.

For a second no one said anything. Bozo bounced on his toes, ready to fight. Frankie Diamond stayed where he was.

Tito gave us supreme stink eye.

Then he burst out laughing. "Hoo, you should see your face! So scared! No worry, liddle punks, you know Tito don't fight wit' weaklings. No make shi-shi pants, everything's cool."

He raised his hands in fake surrender.

All three of them strutted away like

peacocks, banging into each other, laughing their heads off.

My knees felt like jelly. I sucked in a deep breath.

"Man!" Julio said. "Why did you do that? You could've got us killed!"

"That was for Benny."

"Why? He's not even here anymore."

I nodded. "Yeah . . . but I am."

Julio spat. "You're getting as weird as he was, you know?"

I held up karate-chop hands. "Back off, boogaloo! I know kung fu."

After dinner that night, I was in my room with Streak trying to dig up some of Mr. Purdy's writing magic when Mom came in. "Working hard?" she said, closing the door behind her.

"I have to write a one-page paper."

"On what?"

"Ridicule."

Mom's eyebrows went up. "Interesting. I like how your teacher makes you think about things."

I nodded.

Mom had something in her hand. She glanced around my room. "I don't get out here enough."

I shrugged. "I know, it's messy."

She laughed. "That's for sure . . . but it's not what I meant. Anyway, have you seen this?"

She held it out.

I took it.

Clear tape held the two torn pieces of Stella's postcard together.

"Stella asked me to mail it for her," Mom said.

"Huh," I said. Stella had done a good job of taping the postcard back together.

Mom tapped the card with her finger. "Funny, but you and Stella have very similar hand-writing."

I nodded, trying to look surprised. "It's nice she wrote her mom."

"Yes, it is, isn't it?"

I peeked up. Mom gazed into my eyes. "So," she said.

I looked away . . . at my desk.

Mom reached over and picked up the photograph that Benny Obi had given me. "What's this?"

"Um . . . someone gave it to me."

"Who's Benny Obi?"

"A friend . . . at school."

"And he met your dad?"

I nodded. "He saw his show in Las Vegas, I guess with his family."

"That's nice." Mom put the picture back and tugged Stella's postcard from my fingers. "I'll take that."

"Oh . . . sorry."

"I need to lie on the couch with a magazine before this evening gets any stranger."

A while later, Streak and I went outside and stood in the dark listening to the toads down by the river. A sliver of moon hung in the sky, like a clipped fingernail.

I know kung fu.

I smiled and shook my head. "You were something, Benny Obi."

No way in all my life would I ever forget that line, or him. Kung fu or Kung Fu-Fu, or Kung Fooey, who cared? Benny had perked up our lives like the Fourth of July.

In a way, I guess Stella had, too.

I breathed in the cool air and went back into my room. Streak jumped up onto the lower bunk and circled into her spot.

I crawled in and curled around her, with my head propped up in my hand.

"You ever seen a kid with one and a half legs, Streak? Benny did."

She licked my face.

I slept like a rock that night.

And dreamed of driving a big pink car.

A Hawaii Fact:

Ka Lae on the Big Island of Hawaii is the southernmost point in the United States. If you go there, you'll notice a constant wind blowing east to west, 24 hours per day, 365 days per year.

A Calvin Fact:

Sneezing with your eyes open is impossible.

 **Graham Salisbury** is the author of four other Calvin Coconut books: *Trouble Magnet, The Zippy Fix, Dog Heaven,* and *Zoo Breath,* as well as several novels for older readers, including the award-winning *Lord of the Deep, Blue Skin of the Sea, Under the Blood-Red Sun, Eyes of the Emperor, House of the Red Fish,* and *Night of the Howling Dogs.* Graham Salisbury grew up in Hawaii. Calvin Coconut and his friends attend the same school Graham did—Kailua Elementary School. Graham now lives in Portland, Oregon, with his family. Visit him on the Web at grahamsalisbury.com.

 **Jacqueline Rogers** has illustrated more than ninety books for young readers over the past twenty years. She studied illustration at the Rhode Island School of Design. You can visit her at jacquelinerogers.com.